Screwtape
Teaches
The Faith

Screwtape Teaches The Faith

Marlon De La Torre, MA, MEd.

Labora Books
An imprint of Saint Benedict Press
Charlotte, North Carolina

Imprimatur: ✠ Bishop Kevin Vann, JCD, DD
                Bishop of Fort Worth
                August 12, 2011
                Feast of St. Jane Frances de Chantal

ISBN: 978-1-935302-71-1

Cover design by Milo Persic, milo.persic@gmail.com.

Cover images: Demon sneering and sitting in front of a computer and Devil holding trident, © Alashi, iStockphoto.

All Scripture Citations taken from:
Revised Standard Version Bible, Catholic Edition, Copyright ©1952
Division of Christian Churches of the National Council of Churches of Christ in the United States of America
Revised Standard Version Bible, Ignatius Edition, Copyright © 2006
Division of Christian Churches of the National Council of Churches of Christ in the United States of America

All Catechism References taken from:
Catechism of the Catholic Church, 2nd Ed. Copyright ©1997
Libreria Vaticana Editrice

All references from *The Screwtape Letters* taken from:
The Screwtape Letters with Screwtape Proposes a Toast, C.S. Lewis.
Copyright © 1942, Copyright restored ©1996 C.S. Lewis Pte. Ltd. Harper Collins Ed. 2001

Labora Books
An imprint of Saint Benedict Press
Charlotte, North Carolina
2011

To my wife Amy
and my children,
Miguel, Gabriella, and Maria,
the most wonderful gifts a
father could have hoped for.

Table of Contents

Introduction

You have heard the phrase "**the Devil is in the details**" used to describe a certain action or task in need of completion. Or, used in another forum, how missed little details prevented a project from being completed. When involved in this type of situation, the human mind can conjure up so many thoughts and actions out of pure frustration due to the "Devil being in the details." In reality, this is one of the attempts the Devil makes to sway our attention away from Christ and more to our own vices.

St. John Vianney, when presenting a homily on temptation, once wrote:

> It is most unfortunate for ourselves if we do not know that we are tempted in almost all our actions, at one time by pride, by vanity, by the good opinion which we think people should have of us, at another by jealousy, by hatred and by revenge. At other times the Devil comes to us with the foulest and most impure images. You see that even in our prayers he distracts us and turns our minds this way and that.

Screwtape Letters **and the** *Catechism*

Having taught High School catechetics for many years one thing that kept coming up in all of my religious education classes was the issue of sin, temptation, and what to do about it. Go figure, a teenager wanting further explanation on sin, the Devil and how to deal with temptation. This led to the idea of utilizing *The Screwtape Letters* as a required reading for my religious education courses and adding a twist to their lesson. Knowing my classes' keen interest in sin, I decided to construct lesson plans utilizing *The Screwtape Letters* by C.S. Lewis and cross-referencing the chapters with the *Catechism of the Catholic Church*. What I found in this process was a wealth of doctrinal formation that my students instantly gravitated to because they could see the dialogue come alive between Wormwood, the understudy and Screwtape, the uncle, whose instruction dealt with leading souls away from Christ. Using the *Catechism* gave me the opportunity to introduce the students to the *Catechism* and what it is. Once my students figured out how valuable the *Catechism* was in debunking the methods Screwtape taught Wormwood, their secular world view began to change to a Catholic world view.

The value of this curriculum is attributed to sin. Before you start implicating me in inciting heresy, what I mean by this statement is that the value lies in the desire of the human heart to know and understand sin; knowing our concupiscence is something we live with daily. The teenagers I have had the privilege of teaching continually asked me how to avoid sin and seek a closer relationship with Christ. You could see the longing in their eyes for truth that would ease the burden in their souls. With this backdrop, I approached *Screwtape Letters* as an opportunity to help my students know and understand why Christ came into this world.

Sample Backdrop of a Lesson

Book twelve of C.S. Lewis' masterpiece reveals Screwtape encouraging Wormwood to keep "the young man from experiencing reality," in other words, from knowing good and evil. Screwtape tells Wormwood,

> he must be made to imagine that all the
> choices which have effected this change [i.e.
> actions towards God] of course are trivial and
> revocable. He must not be allowed to suspect
> that he is now, however slowly, heading right
> away from the sun on a line which will carry
> him into the cold and dark of utmost space.

This poignant statement reflects the desire to keep man from understanding truth, and the love God has for all of his children. In another way, Screwtape is encouraging a relativistic worldview for this young man. Screwtape tells Wormwood;

> As long as he retains externally the habits of
> a Christian life he can still be made to think
> of himself as one who has adopted a few new
> friends and amusements but whose spiritual
> state is much the same as it was six weeks ago.

Debunking Screwtape

The process to "debunk" Screwtape involved selecting a passage from the book and then carefully finding the counterpoints to Screwtape via the *Catechism*, e.g.

> Sin is an offense against reason, truth, and
> right conscience; it is a failure of genuine love
> for God and neighbor caused by a perverse
> attachment to certain goods (CCC 1849).

The aim of catechesis is to seek what is above, not what is below. (*Col* 3:1-3) Our human will can only carry us so far by our own merits. We cannot forget who gave us our soul, God, for the sole purpose of directing our very being to worship Him and receive His love. The moral law is the work of God's instruction for our lives. It is His fatherly instruction that guides us to take care of our souls. It prescribes for man the ways, rules of conduct that lead to the promised beatitude; it proscribes the ways of evil which turn him away from God and His love (CCC 1950).

Application of the *Catechism*

The moral law should not be viewed as a spiritual chain around your neck preventing you from experiencing freedom. In the moral law true freedom resonates in every action we commit. If we embrace the moral law, then we embrace Christ who is the end of the law, that everyone who has faith may be justified (*Rom* 10:4). One profound effect resulting from this catechetical activity was my students' realization of the reality of sin. Keep in mind, these students did not become paranoid or scrupulous with respect to every sinful act. They went from a desensitized notion of sin to the reality that sin unfortunately is alive and well. They did not view sin as a mistake or error in judgment. If it's a sin, then it's a sin.

The outline described above reveals how powerful the *Catechism* can be when used to our advantage in instructing others in the faith. The purpose of the story of Screwtape and Wormwood, at first glance intriguing, is unveiled more when paralleled with the *Catechism*. Why? Because one sees the classic battle line of good versus evil and the purpose of the Crucifixion, to help us see true love and realize this love comes from Christ.

Important Catechetical Documents

Here are the major documents of the Church appropriate for the ministry of Catechesis and Religious Education in the Catholic Church.

CCC   *Catechism of the Catholic Church*, 2nd Edition
Libreria Vaticana Editrice, 1997.

CT   *Catechesi Tradendae*
Pope John Paul II, Apostolic Exhortation, 1979.

EN   *On Evangelization In the Modern World*
Pope Paul VI, 1975.

GDC *The General Directory for Catechesis*
Sacred Congregation for the Clergy, 1997

How this Resource Works

Any budding catechist who desires to teach the Catholic faith well will realize the key to sound instruction is to teach the basics. If you teach the basics by keeping to the sources of Catholic instruction, i.e. Sacred Tradition and Sacred Scripture, then they will realize how important the *Catechism of the Catholic Church* is.

This resource is meant to bring together two wonderful and significant resources in our path to Heaven. *The Screwtape Letters* will forever engage the hearts and minds of anyone who reads it. Whether they believe in God or not, they will see that a certain symphony exists between good and evil. There are good acts and evil ones. In reality it is that simple when the intellect has a full understanding of the two. C.S. Lewis was masterful in his expression of Screwtape and Wormwood. The *Catechism of the Catholic Church* serves as the definitive synthesis of the Catholic faith. In summary, the whole of the Deposit of Faith, i.e. all that the Church teaches and professes in Jesus Christ, is found in this harmony of love called the *Catechism*.

The *Catechism*, when its content is extrapolated to enhance the overall comprehension of the faith to others, becomes a tool of instruction and conversion. At its core, it serves as a tool of evangelization par excellence. Noting that the foundation of the *Catechism* is rooted in Sacred Scripture, that is, scripture drives doctrinal teaching, the *Catechism* takes on greater significance because it "houses" so to speak the "Deposit of Faith."

Within the context of this resource, the emphasis must come back to explaining "the story", i.e. Salvation History. Why do we profess faith in Jesus Christ? Ultimately, this becomes the fundamental instruction piece all must see. Jesus Christ came not only to restore our souls to God the Father, but He also came to restore our dignity as children of God. Sin, introduced by the free will of our parents, created a chasm of uncertainty in our relationship with God. Of all the common characteristics Abraham, Isaac, Jacob, and Moses share, one is very striking, they are called to move the people of God closer to Him.

Hence, this is the situation we encounter every time we engage those we teach. Introduction to the love of God takes time to embrace, especially when those engaged have not been properly disposed to receive it. This resource is a means to open the doors to those who desire to receive the love that never ends (CCC 25).

Structure

First Step

The first step in using this resource is prayer. The letter to the Hebrews reminds us that: Faith is the assurance of things hoped for, the conviction of things not seen (*Heb.* 11:1-2). Ask for assistance as you prepare to engage souls who are genuinely looking for some semblance of truth. Remember, it's not only what you teach; it's how you witness that doctrine to others. In other words, are you living the doctrine you're teaching? Preparation is important for catechetical success. Utilize key resources for example, Sacred Scripture, The *Catechism of the Catholic Church*, Sacred Art, beautiful music, etc.

Second Step

Each chapter from *The Screwtape Letters* is summarized with one main theme the chapter describes. This theme is drawn out in reference to what Screwtape directs Wormwood to do in encouraging his patient away from God. Read this theme carefully as it will guide you towards application of the lesson. Keep in mind that each chapter of *The Screwtape*

Letters is short and filled with other relevant material. For the sake of brevity I have only concentrated on one main theme per chapter (book). There are several themes the catechist can draw from.

Third Step

Carefully read how to debunk Screwtape and his understudy Wormwood. You will see an outline of the *Catechism* in reference to the main theme of each chapter. Here is where you provide a sound explanation through the *Catechism* on rebuking Screwtape.

Fourth Step

The application of the *Catechism* shows the catechist how to apply the *Catechism* in daily life, especially in the lives of the students we teach.

Fifth Step

Pray for successful instruction through the power of the Holy Spirit. Review the content studied via Sacred Scripture and the *Catechism*. Your aim is to get the student to see the development of sin and how we can refute the Devil's canny ways through the Deposit of Faith.

Chapter

Faith and Relativism

*"By faith man completely submits his intellect and
his will to God."*   —Dei Verbum, 5

General Theme

Chapter one reflects a classic battle line that all human
beings face; relativism, which leads towards an avoidance of
a doctrinal creed. Screwtape guides Wormwood to keep his
patient off-balance by exposing the patient to a more lethal
approach, e.g. *relativism.* This thought process is meant to
make the patient regard doctrine as inconsequential. Further-
ing this point is the *notion to avoid seeking the truth behind
doctrine by "jargon" and not by reasoned argument.*

The attempt is to sway the individual from genuinely
seeking truth. Chapter one reflects an attempt to refrain from
developing an authentic faith. There is an emphasis to have
the human mind continually think of things outside of reality,
thus the question of doctrine becomes a moot point. Keep in
mind, man regardless of his state in life, is continually seeking
truth in some way or form.

Debunking Screwtape

So, where do we begin? Essentially, you take the position of faith. All human beings are created to profess the Divine. More specifically, we are called to profess our Worship to the one true God. The *Catechism* reminds us the obedience of faith means to "hear or listen to," "to submit freely to the word that has been heard" (CCC 144).

Relativism, in a general sense reflects the desire to discredit faith as a reasonable position from which to answer questions. Faith reflects our "personal adherence to God" (CCC 150). The key in debunking someone with Screwtape tendencies is to pose the position of faith as a genuine quality every human being has. This is not a question to engage Gnosticism for the sole purpose of being content with any knowledge. The emphasis here is a true faith rooted in genuine reason.

> "But I am not ashamed, for I know whom I have believed, and I am sure that he is able to guard until that Day what has been entrusted to me" —(*2 Tim* 1:12).

Application of the Catechism

The *Catechism* provides us with a wonderful summary of doctrine/dogma found in section 88. The Church's Magisterium exercises the authority it holds from Christ to the fullest extent when it defines dogmas, that is, when it proposes, in a form obliging the Christian people to an unquestionable adherence of faith. Doctrine, by its very nature develops for the purpose of discovering further truth from the original source. When teaching this first chapter, it is important to draw the natural connection of love God has for His children and the gifts He has left for us, mainly through His Son Jesus Christ to revoke any relativistic notion that nothing matters. Revealing the value of doctrine is essential because its composition comes from Christ. The students you teach must receive doctrine as an instruction in love. If we look at the Apostles Creed, it consists of many "I believe" statements. These statements or professions of faith aim to impart to the student the ability to recognize a creedal language whose sole purpose is to foster a genuine capacity to love through faith and reason.

Recommended Scripture References:

- *Mk* 16:15
- *Jn* 8:31-32—dogmas shed light on our faith

Recommended Catechism References:

- CCC 88–90
- CCC 888–889

Vocabulary:

Relativism—the belief that what is "right" or "wrong" is not absolute and can vary according to circumstances.

Doctrine—the teachings of the Catholic Church founded by Jesus Christ himself. We are called to follow and live these truths revealed by Christ found through Sacred Scripture and the teaching authority of the Church.

Chapter

2

Bearing False Witness and Authentic Conversion

"At that time Jesus declared, I thank you, Father,
Lord of Heaven and earth, that you have hidden
these things from the wise and understanding and
revealed them to infants; yes, Father for such was
your gracious will."   —*Mt* 11:25–26

General Theme

Screwtape is very displeased that "Wormwood's patient"
has become Christian. However, Screwtape is not worried
because he knows many who have become Christian essentially fall back to their state of life as before, meaning their
conversion either was not genuine or not properly instructed.
The main theme in this chapter is the reference to *bearing*
false witness against your neighbor. The problem is that the
patient starts seeing the negative in those around him. Even
though the "patient" has become Christian, those around him

do not appear to have the same zeal as he does. This is exactly what Screwtape wants, to create disillusionment about the Christian people the patient sees, and thereby foster a disappointment in his Christian faith.

Debunking Screwtape

Genuine conversion is a grace given to us by God. In Jesus Christ we have the Word made flesh that sanctifies and anchors a reality that Jesus is real and did indeed sacrifice himself for our salvation. The *Catechism* reminds us that Faith:

- Is a human act
- Is possible only by the grace and the interior help of the Holy Spirit
- Belief is vital towards this end (CCC 154).

In other words, faith, if it's honestly sought, demands to see truth, even when the truth around the person is not pretty. Christ is still present amongst us in the Liturgy. Keep in mind, the liturgy is a public work (CCC 1069) which means it calls us to proclaim a living faith in participation with God. Just because those around us are not participating, does not mean we shouldn't either.

Application of the Catechism

The *Catechism* reminds us that we should not bear false witness against our neighbor (CCC 2464). The Eighth Commandment is given to us so that we do not misrepresent the truth about others. Our responsibility is to bear witness to the truth even when others do not.

"It was said to the men of old, "You shall not
swear falsely, but shall perform to the Lord
what you have sworn"   —(*Mt* 5:33).

We are called to moral uprightness. When we experience
conversion, our call is to seek truth, beauty and goodness. No
one wants a bad tasting meal. You prefer a meal that satisfies
the senses. This same premise is tied to our faith. When we
break the Eighth Commandment we are saying our preference
is a bad meal versus a delicious one.

"The Christian is not to be ashamed then of
testifying to our Lord"   —(*2 Tim* 1:8).

We are called to do the following:

- Take part in the life of the Church i.e. the Mass

- Act as witness of the Gospel—i.e. live an active prayer
life

- Transmit the faith in word and deed i.e. spiritual and
corporal works of mercy (CCC 2472).

Recommended Scripture References

- *2 Tim* 1:8

- *Mt* 5:33

- *Mt* 11:25–26

Recommended *Catechism* References

- CCC 154–156
- CCC 2464–2492

Vocabulary

Faith—is a gift from God and an act of the will wherein the person firmly believes the truths which God has revealed.

Works of Mercy—acts done to help our neighbors, e.g. spiritual works—praying for the dead, forgiving, instructing in faith; corporal—feeding the hungry, clothing the naked, visiting the sick etc.

Chapter 3

Honor Thy Self or Honor God

*"Do you not know that you are God's temple, and
that God's spirit dwells in you? If anyone destroys
God's temple, God will destroy him. For God's
temple is holy, and that temple you are"*

—*1 Cor* 3:16–17

General Theme

Screwtape encourages Wormwood to destroy the relationship between his patient and his patient's mother.
Wormwood's biggest fear is the work of Christ from within
and from without. What this means is the ability for mother
and son to draw on an intimate relationship with Jesus Christ
(*Jn* 14:6; *1 Jn* 1:1–4).

Another main theme in this chapter is Screwtape's
emphasis to Wormwood to keep the young man's mind on
the inner life. Wormwood should encourage the young man
to think that he is the reason for his own conversion journey,

without an interior understanding of Christ. In other words, distort the understanding of having a personal relationship with Jesus Christ. Screwtape continues his instruction by encouraging Wormwood to keep "his [the patient's] mind off the most elementary duties, by directing him to think of the most advanced ones. This means Wormwood must keep his patient's mind way from the simplicity of loving Christ and instead find a morally relative alternative to distract him.

Debunking Screwtape

Our inner life is rooted in Christ, and leads us to an examination of our relationship with Christ (CCC 1454, See: *Mt* 5–7; *Rom* 12–15; *1 Cor* 12–13). Jesus calls us to conversion. The call is an essential part of the proclamation of the Kingdom of God (CCC 1427).

Interior repentance is a radical orientation of our whole life, a return, a conversion to God with all our heart, an end of sin, a turning away from evil (CCC 1431); conversion is a work of grace and makes our hearts return to him (CCC 1432).

Application of the *Catechism*

Screwtape does not want this young man to discover God (See CCC 51-53 on the revelation of God).

We can draw upon the Fourth Commandment: honor your father and your mother (CCC 2197-2200). Specifically, the Fourth Commandment emphasizes charity directed to our parents, in its proper order, after God. In essence, it is honoring the family as the root of civilization.

The *Catechism* reminds us:

- that the Fourth Commandment is directed to children in their relationship with their parents
  Why? Because this relationship is universal (CCC 2199).

- that parents are also called to be teachers, instructors, witnesses of the faith.

- that Jesus calls us to conversion. The call is an essential part of the proclamation of the Kingdom of God (CCC 1427).

- that interior repentance is a radical orientation of our whole life, a return, a conversion to God with all our heart, an end of sin, a turning away from evil (CCC 1431).

- that conversion is a work of grace and makes our hearts return to Him (CCC 1432).

Note: There is an obvious direct emphasis to ignore truth, beauty, and goodness in God's creatures. Man is limited by what he sees, versus what is unseen. In other words, the perceived visible reality; a birthmark, or a physical limitation; a limp, loss of an arm, crooked teeth, tends to be viewed rather than the invisible reality; the soul of the human being.

Remember: God loved us so much, He sent His only begotten Son to literally take upon himself the sins of humanity. This point echoes why the Word became flesh:

1. In order to save us by reconciling us with God (CCC 457; *1 Jn* 4:10; 4:14; 3:5).

2. In order so that we might know God's love (CCC 458; *Jn* 3:16).

3. In order to be our model of holiness (CCC 459; *Mt* 11:29; *Jn* 14:6).

4. In order to be partakers of the Divine Nature (CCC 460; *2 Pet* 1:4).

The *Catechism* reminds us:

Our Christian Beatitude calls us to:

- embrace and prepare for the coming of the Kingdom of God (*Mt* 4:17), meaning always be prepared through your Christian charity towards others.

- embrace the vision of God: "Blessed are the pure of heart, for they shall see God (*Mt* 5:8; *1 Jn* 2:1; *1 Cor* 13:12).

- enter into the joy of the Lord (*Mt* 25:21–23).

- enter into God's rest (*Heb* 4:7–11).

Our Human freedom rests in reason and will (CCC 1731).

- To act or not to act

- Human freedom is a force for growth and maturity in truth and goodness; it attains its perfection when directed toward God, our beatitude.

As long as freedom has not bound itself definitively to its ultimate good which is God, there is the possibility of choosing between evil and good, and thus growing in perfection or failing and sinning (CCC 1732).

Recommended Scripture References:

- *Rom* 12:15
- *Mt* 25:21-23
- *Jn* 14:6
- *2 Pet* 1:4

Recommended *Catechism* References

- CCC 1427-1433
- CCC 2197-2199
- CCC 456-460

Vocabulary

Beatitude—he teachings of Jesus on the Sermon on the Mount. The beatitudes serve as a reflection of the Ten Commandments and their application.

Revelation—God communicating himself by revealing His divine plan to all humanity.

Human Freedom—the exercise of the free will given to man by God.

Chapter

Authentic Prayer

*"For me prayer is a surge of the heart; it is a
simple look turned toward heaven, it is a cry
of recognition and of love, embracing both
trial and joy.*   —St. Therese of Lisieux

General Theme

Screwtape takes the time to discuss the painful subject
of prayer with Wormwood. In this chapter, the intent of the
devils is **to keep the "patient" from developing an authentic
prayer life.** This serves as the main theme. Another important
note is that if the "patient" does develop a prayer life, Wormwood should make sure it is not centered on God, but rather
on "idols". The object for Wormwood is to keep the "patient"
from walking with God.

Debunking Screwtape

Prayer is painful to the Devil. It leads toward a deeper

communication with God and develops a barrier between man and the Devil. Screwtape desires confusion, complacency, and indifference towards a journey with Jesus Christ. Prayer is a genuine conversation with God. The desire is open communication to God's grace (CCC 2559). An outline of the battle between Screwtape and Christ on prayer may look something like this:

- "I"-centered prayer vs. Christ-centered prayer.

- Superficial holiness vs. interior holiness

- There is a direct fear against intercessory and contemplative prayer, i.e. silent prayer-meditation. An example would be Lectio Divina.

> *"Prayer is a raising of one's mind and heart to*
> *God or the requesting of good things from God."*
> —St. John Damascene

Application of the *Catechism*

There are three principal parables to prayer: CCC 2613

1. The importunate friend (*Lk* 11:5-13) invites us to urgent prayer. Knock and it will be opened to you.

2. The importunate widow (*Lk* 18:1-8); it is necessary to pray always without ceasing and with the patience of faith.

3. The Pharisee and the tax collector (*Lk* 18:9–14); this concerns the humility of the heart that prays: "God, be merciful to me a sinner." Kyrie eleison—Lord have mercy.

The Catechism reminds us:

Adoration is the first attitude of man acknowledging that he is a creature before his Creator. It exalts the greatness of the Lord who made us (*Ps* 95:1-6), and the almighty power of the Savior who sets us free from evil.

Adoration is the homage of the spirit to the King of Glory (*Ps* 24: 9-10); respectful silence in the presence of the "ever greater" God.

Key phrase from Screwtape: It is funny how mortals always picture us as putting things into their minds: in reality our best work is done by keeping things out (Lewis 1942, 16).

1. Screwtape desires to translate prayer into a communication with the self and not with Christ.

2. The Devil views prayer as a weapon against His invitations to souls.

3. The Devil fears prayer because it calls upon the action of Christ to intercede on behalf of the soul.

4. Prayer calls upon immediate action from God, something Screwtape does not want.

Screwtape reminds Wormwood that he has a subtler weapon against man that provides misdirection in prayer.

- The weapon is the lack of man's ability to see everything through the eyes (lens) of Christ.

- Screwtape fears devotion and devotionals, especially sacred art.

- His greater fear is the Incarnation. The Incarnation

brings to human reality the saving realities of God through his son Jesus Christ (*Jn* 6:52 ff).

The *Catechism* reminds us:

There are certain Characteristics of the people of God:

- We are part of a chosen race, a holy nation (*1 Pet* 2:9).

- We enter into the kingdom through our Baptism.

- Jesus Christ is our head, anointed for every good work.

- We are called to display the dignity and freedom of the sons of God.

- To live the commandment of love (*Jn* 13:34).

- Be the salt of the earth (*Mt* 5:13-16).

- Our journey to Heaven is a preparation.

The ultimate form of prayer is the "Our Father"

- It is the summary of the whole Gospel (CCC 2761).

- It is the center of the Church (CCC 2762-2764).

    "The Lord's Prayer is the most perfect of prayers ..." —St. Thomas Aquinas

Recommended Scripture Passages:

- *Lk* 11:5–13

- *Lk* 18:1–8

- *Mt* 21:13

- *Acts* 1:14

- *Acts* 2:39–42
- *Col* 4:2

Recommended *Catechism* references:

- CCC 2569
- CCC 2558–2565
- CCC 2566–2567
- CCC 2599–2602
- CCC 2626–2643

Vocabulary

Prayer—preparing your heart and mind to God in praise.

Praise—prayer of recognition to God.

Adoration—Acknowledging God as God, Creator, and Lord of all.

Lord's Prayer—the title early Christians gave to prayer which Jesus entrusted to his disciples and to the Church CCC 2759).

Chapter 5

Despair and Hope

"For in this hope we were saved. Now hope that is seen is not hope. For who hopes for what he sees? But if we hope for what we do not see, we wait for it with patience." —*Rom* 8:24–25

General Theme

Screwtape warns Wormwood not to assume that a man is in despair solely based upon his actions. Meaning, just because man may not see hope at first, it does not mean he will not see hope later. He knows that the virtue of Hope may all of a sudden lead the "patient" away from Despair. Screwtape uses the backdrop of war and suffering as weapons to perpetuate despair. Yet, **a more fearful characteristic in the eyes of Screwtape is man's ability to take an act of suffering and equate it to Christ and the Redemption of humanity through Christ's Crucifixion thus elevating the virtue of Hope to a position above his.**

Debunking Screwtape

The sin of Despair holds weight only when man thinks there is nothing to the contrary. God makes himself known through the creation of us, his children. Our very existence gives us hope because He loves us so much as to give us the opportunity to worship Him and only Him (CCC 2084–2085). The First Commandment serves as the backdrop to the virtue of Hope. Screwtape offers no sound alternative, only continual confusion. Hope is the confident expectation of divine blessing and the beatific vision of God (CCC 2090); our desire rests in seeing God face to face in Heaven. There is an end journey of the earthly life and a perpetual intimacy of the soul united with the Father in Heaven.

Application of the *Catechism*

Tied to the First Commandment—"You shall worship the one true God"—hope, is nestled intimately with the journey of our Redemption through the Father and the Son (CCC 2084; CCC 571). The Paschal Mystery reflects the great lengths Jesus Christ took to brings us to the love of the Father. The Son of God became flesh in order to know God's love (CCC 458).

Despair is the abandonment of hope in salvation and in the forgiveness of sins (CCC 2091). Understanding the grace of suffering and its link to Redemption reveals a love unique between a Father and His Children. In other words, we are loved.

The aim of the catechist in this particular chapter is to reveal to the student how much God does indeed love us. A common trait of despair is the assumption there is no love. Knowing this assumption to be false, revealing the beauty of worshipping the one true God will manifest a longing towards what this love entails. Hence:

> "The Son of God who came down from heaven, not to do [his] own will, but the will of him who sent [him], said on coming into the world, 'Lo I have come to do your will, O God.' And by that will we have been sanctified through the offering of the body of Jesus Christ once for all. From the first moment of his Incarnation the Son embraces the Father's plan of divine salvation in his redemptive mission:' My food is to do the will of him who sent me, and to accomplish his work"
>
> —(CCC 606).

Recommended Scripture References

- *Rom* 8:24–25
- *Rom* 5:2–3
- *1 Cor* 13:13

Recommended *Catechism* References

- CCC 606
- CCC 2084–2085
- CCC 2090–2091
- CCC 571; 458

Vocabulary

Despair—man does not see salvation from God nor does he believe that his sins can be forgiven.

Redemption—Jesus Christ's redemptive acts e.g. his Crucifixion to ransom us from our sins in order to be slaves of sin.

Hope—our desire and expectation of grace from God in this life and the next.

Chapter **6**

Fear of the Lord vs. Fear itself

> *"And in the fourth watch of the night he came to them, walking on the sea. But when the disciples saw him walking on the sea, they were terrified, saying, 'It is a ghost!' And they cried out for fear. But immediately he spoke to them, saying, 'Take heart, it is I; have no fear.'"*   *Mt* 14: 25–27

General Theme

Screwtape encourages Wormwood to present suffering not as a grace or a cross to endure but as something to fear. That is; if the "patient" views his cross with fear outside of God's love, then there is nothing to gain in God's grace. The "patient" takes his burdens onto himself and does not seek the assistance of God through prayer.

This mindset leads a person confronted with a difficult challenge, to dwell on the challenge more than seeking God's assistance in the matter.

Debunking Screwtape

Suffering is clearly defined by the virtue of love. We see this in the Crucifixion of our Lord. He offered Himself, taking the form of a slave to save us from our own faults, i.e. sins.

"You know that you were ransomed from the futile ways inherited from your fathers, not with perishable things such as silver or gold, but with the precious blood of Christ, like that of a lamb without blemish or spot. He was destined before the foundation of the world but was made manifest at the end of the times for your sake" (*1 Pt* 1:18–20).

When speaking about suffering, we cannot undo the Crucifixion. The path to our final home in Heaven was dependent upon this free act of Christ. This free act displayed a perfect form of love.

Application of the *Catechism*

Christ came to do the will of the Father (CCC 606). His intention was to bring us out of our sinful paths. When we experience hardship, our first inclination is to avoid any pain associated with the hardship. Our concupiscence, i.e. inclination to sin, blinds us from truly embracing this hardship (cross) as a gift from God. Grace serves as a free gift from God to deepen our relationship with Him.

The cross is the unique sacrifice of Christ, the "one mediator between God and men" (CCC 618). He calls his disciples to take up their cross and follow him (*Mt* 16:24; CCC 618).

"Apart from the cross there is no other ladder
by which we may get to heaven."

—St. Rose of Lima

Recommended Scripture References

- *Mt* 14:25–27
- *1 Tim* 2:5
- *1 Tim* 1:18–21
- *Heb* 5:9
- *Is* 53:11
- *Acts* 3:14

Recommended *Catechism* References

- CCC 601
- CCC 618–620
- CCC 1763–1766

Vocabulary

Redemption—Christ's salvific work on the Cross, i.e.
His Crucifixion represents the salvation of mankind
from the slavery of sin.

Suffering—to endure hardship and struggle.

Cross—the instrument used to kill Christ. It is a
unique symbol representing Christ's unique sacrifice
and his role as mediator between God and man.

Chapter 7

ᴀ Wolf in Sheep's Clothing

> *"The tongue is an unrighteous world among our*
> *members, staining the whole body, setting on fire*
> *the cycle of nature, and set on fire by hell. . . With*
> *it we bless the Lord and Father, and with it we*
> *curse men, who are made in the likeness of God.*
> *From the same mouth come blessing and cursing."*
> —James 3:6–7

General Theme

It's all relative, so to speak. Screwtape reminds Worm-wood that ignorance of the existence of God is a good thing. However, if [they] are able to convince man that God is really just an illusion of sorts, then man's attention will turn to other worldly, i.e. idolatrous desires, such as "the worship of sex" (Lewis 1942, 31). Screwtape's intention with Wormwood is to have the "patient" find an **alternative to God** and view the Devil as a normal part of society that is inconsequential. Hence, this serves as the main theme. Screwtape furthers his instruction with Wormwood by telling him that "all extremes, except extreme devotion to the enemy (Jesus) are to be encouraged" (Lewis 1942, 32).

Debunking Screwtape

Screwtape neglects one important point when attempting to sway man's capacity to know and love God. God is the author of creation, i.e. the world and humanity. Man contains a natural created inclination to worship God. The world and the human person provide a fundamental reason to believe God is not an allusion (CCC 31-34).

> The human person: With his openness to truth and beauty, his sense of moral goodness, his freedom and the voice of his conscience, with his longings for the infinite and for happiness, man questions himself about God's existence (CCC 33).

Essentially there is a first cause. That is, through reason there is a clear understanding that there is something greater in the world than our own physical presence.

Application of the *Catechism*

The First Commandment provides a reasonable direction towards understanding the wolf in sheep's clothing scenario. This expression aptly describes the Devil's method of operation. It is no coincidence that the First Commandment of God is to worship the Lord your God and him only shall you serve (CCC 2084; *Ex* 20:2-5; *Mt* 4:10). God knew our tendencies to venture away from Him when the situation became uncomfortable (See the Golden Calf, Ex: 32).

When we firmly assent our belief in God, we express our faith, hope, and love in Him (CCC 2086–2089). A sound way of affirming God's presence is the practice of adoring God. He is our Alpha and Omega, the beginning and the end.

> Adoration is the first act of the virtue of religion. To adore God is to acknowledge him as God, as the Creator and Savior, the Lord and Master of everything that exists, as infinite and merciful love —(CCC 2096).

Taking the first three commandments, the individual regardless of reasonable age where the intellect and will are exercised, can see the value of worshipping the one true God, keeping His name holy and worshipping Him in proper order.

Recommended Scripture References

- *Mt* 10:27
- *Ex* 20:2–5
- *Mt* 4:10
- *James* 3:6–7

Recommended *Catechism* References

- CCC 31–34
- CCC 2084–2090

- CCC 2096
- CCC 199–202

Vocabulary

Worship—adoration and honor given to God. This serves as our first act of public worship (CCC 2096).

Creed—a summation resulting in a profession of faith in God e.g. "I believe."

Ten Commandment—the ten laws given by God to Moses and the people of Israel.

Chapter 8

Bad Habits

*"And you he made alive, when you were dead
through the trespasses and sins in which you once
walked, following the course of this world, following the prince of power of the air, the spirit that is
now at work in the sons of disobedience."*

Eph 2:1–2

General Theme

Screwtapes cautions Wormwood not to rest on the "patient's" religious phase dying away (Lewis 1942, 37). There is another step to take with this individual. It centers on the **"Law of Undulation"** (Lewis 1942, 37). The Law of Undulation refers to the fact that "while [a human's] spirit can be directed to an eternal object, [his] body, passions, and imaginations are in continual change." This is because he lives in time and not in eternity, as the spirits do. Therefore, he will experience times of spiritual dryness and times of spiritual consolation, and even if his will is always fixed on God, his emotions and behavior will not always show it. Screwtape tells Wormwood if he had watched his patient carefully, he would have noticed that undulation or inconsistent feelings impact every part of his life.

God desires a relationship with His children, something Screwtape loathes. The Devil wants control of the "patient's" will.

Debunking Screwtape

Screwtape underestimates the power of virtue and its effect on man. He continually emphasizes the "patient's" weakness and emptiness as his food against the enemy. But man has the ability to exercise his free will to love God even when he does not feel inclined to do so. He has the power to remain faithful, even during periods of dryness or fatique which the Law of Undulation assures he will experience. This constancy and fidelity in the midst of changing emotions creates a habit (or virtue) of loving God regardless of feelings. Freedom is the power, rooted in reason and will, to act or not to act, to do this or that, and so to perform deliberate actions on one's own responsibility (CCC 1731).

> Freedom makes man responsible for his acts
> to the extent that they are voluntary. Progress
> in virtue, knowledge of the good, and ascesis
> (practice of penance, mortification and self-
> denial) enhance the mastery of the will over its
> acts (CCC 1734).

Application of the Catechism

Every human act has one or the other characteristic. It is either good or bad (CCC 1749). Morally speaking, the human act is judged upon the fundamental truth that man is a moral subject based on his freedom to act. The key to all this is the exercise of the will to act. The Catechism reminds us that virtue is a habitual disposition to do the good. It allows the person not only to perform good acts, but to give the best of himself (CCC 1803).

In other words all of us have the capacity to avoid sin. By exercising virtue in its basic form, a desire to do well, man has the ability to emerge from habitual acts or pleasures that draw us away from Christ and His love and form habits that make us more like Christ.

> "The goal of a virtuous life is to become like
> God."   —St. Gregory of Nyssa

A bad habit, whether it be a lack of prayer due to watching too much television, or swearing, can be altered by a genuine desire to embrace a virtuous demeanor and draw the intellect and will to act according to our faith in God. The moral virtues are acquired by human effort. They are the fruit of repeated morally good acts; they dispose all the powers of the human being for communion with divine love (CCC 1804).

The **Four Cardinal Virtues** (CCC 1805–1809) serve as the catalyst for breaking vicious habits leading a person away from God's love. Prudence, temperance, fortitude, and justice serve as the beacons of hope for living a virtuous life and avoiding the habits of the flesh aimed to draw us away from Christ and His love.

Recommended Scripture References

- *Eph* 2:1–2
- *Phil* 4:8
- *1 Pet* 4:7
- *Col* 4:1
- *Jn* 16:33

Recommended *Catechism* References

- CCC 1731–1734
- CCC 1805–1809
- CCC 1749

Vocabulary

Virtue—the disposition for man to perform good acts

Morality of the human act—depends upon the object, the intent and the circumstance; these three points make up the morality of the human act.

Freedom—the responsibility man takes for his own acts.

Cardinal Virtues—pivotal human virtues stabilizing the intellect and will in governing our acts in accordance with our faith and reason.

Chapter

Spiritual Dryness, Sexual Temptation, and Dignity of the Human Person

"In their case the god of this world has blinded the minds of the unbelievers, to keep them from seeing the light of the Gospel of the glory of Christ, who is the likeness of God."   2 Cor 4:3–4

General Theme

Screwtape reminds Wormwood that **spiritual dryness, i.e. spiritual undulation "provides an excellent opportunity for all sensual temptations, particularly those of sex"** (Lewis 1942, 43). Screwtape maintains that in order to bring man away from authentic spiritual intimacy with Christ, Wormwood should attack "man's inner world" when it is drab, cold, and empty. The relationship here is that spiritual emptiness allows man to seek gratification in unholy sexual ways. To fill a void through sexual gratification outside of the holy bonds of Matrimony is exactly what the devils want. Thus, an unhealthy view of sex is, in the Devil's mind, a tool to pervert the soul of man.

Debunking Screwtape

Screwtape concedes that natural pleasure, in particular those experienced by man in a physical sense were created by God. The aim of Screwtape is to have "the patient" engaged in these pleasures in a way God does not intend. Man was created in the image and likeness of God. The virtue of humility serves as a sound weapon against man's spiritual dryness.

> In positive terms, the battle against the possessive and dominating self requires vigilance and sobriety of heart (CCC 2730).

Application of the *Catechism*

The *Catechism* tells us that dryness is intimately associated with contemplation when the heart is separated from God. This is the moment of sheer faith (CCC 2731). When you parallel this understanding with the morality of human acts, the intellect and will of man is called a Christian intimacy rooted in Christ first. Sexual lustful desires lack a foundational fidelity if exercised outside the bonds of holy matrimony; sexual intercourse is an act solely for the intimate union between man and woman in marriage. It is a mutual giving of two persons for the good of children and each other. This demands fidelity (CCC 1646). Fidelity to a spouse in Holy Matrimony reflects fidelity to God the Father.

We must not forget, as creatures created in the image and likeness of God, we are called to hold the moral standard

(CCC 1950). The Moral Law presupposes the rational order, established among creatures for their good and to serve their final end by the power, wisdom, and goodness of God (CCC 1951).

"Thy will be done," this important petition of the Our Father calls us to discern the will of God and obtain the endurance to do it (*Rom* 12:2). Jesus teaches us that one enters the kingdom of heaven not by speaking words, but by doing the will of the Father in Heaven (*Mt* 7:21; CCC 2827).

Recommended Scripture References

- *Lk* 15: 1–32 (Prodigal Son)
- *Col* 1:13
- *2 Cor* 4:3–4
- *Mt* 7:21
- *Rom* 12:2

Recommended *Catechism* References

- CCC 2730-2731
- CCC 1951
- CCC 2827
- CCC 1646

Vocabulary

Morality—the goodness or evil of human acts. Morality of a human Act depends on the object, intent, and circumstance.

Beatitude—Blessedness and happiness toward heaven (CCC 1024).

Nature—refers to human nature, though sounded and weakened by sin, still continues to participate in God's creative work (CCC 405).

Chapter 10

A Well Informed Moral Conscience?

*"So they are without excuse, for although they
knew God they did not honor him as God or
give thanks to him, but they became futile in
their thinking and their senseless minds were
darkened."* —Rom 1:20–21

General Theme

The main theme of this chapter is to **be wary who your
friends are**. Screwtape encourages Wormwood to foster
the "patient's" relationships with individuals that draw him
away from the enemy. One way is to help him realize that
his Christian faith proves to be in direct conflict with his
new friends. The question becomes the choice he will make
in regarding these friends. What the "patient" is challenged
with is whether to follow his moral conscience and move
away from these friends or to ignore his moral conscience all

together, and keep them. Screwtape tells Wormwood: "As long as the postponement lasts he will be in a false position" (Lewis 1942, 50).

Debunking Screwtape

Human beings are fallible. True friendship is not rooted in man but in man's relationship with Jesus Christ. Friendship must take on a genuine Christ-centered approach. Man's capacity to make right judgments rests in his ability to have a well informed conscience. Screwtape underestimated man's ability to seek good amidst a world of evil. For man has in his head a law inscribed by God (CCC 1776).

Application of the *Catechism*

Moral conscience is present at the heart of every person. It engages man at the appropriate moment to do good and to avoid evil (CCC 1777).

Characteristics of a moral conscience:

- It judges particular choices

- It approves good choices

- It denounces evil choices

- It bears witness to the authority of truth in the supreme good to which man is drawn

- It welcomes the commandments (CCC 1777).

> *Return to your conscience, question it ... Turn*
> *inward, brethren and in everything you do, see*
> *God as your witness.* —St. Augustine

Conscience reflects a proper judgment of reason associated with human acts. Man's call is to perform acts within a proper moral outlook. The Divine law is not recognized unless man's conscience is directed to God. The dignity of the human person implies and requires uprightness of moral conscience. Conscience includes perceiving the principles of morality. (CCC 1780).

Conscience enables man to assume responsibility for the acts performed. Man is free to make morally conscience acts in a well-informed enlightened manner.

A properly informed conscience:

- Acts in truth

- Seeks the dignity of the human person

- Exercises Prudence

- Uses the Word of God (Sacred Scripture) as a light for the journey. See: Psalm 119:105

Recommended Scripture References:

- *Rom* 1:31–32

- *Psalm* 119:105

- *Rom* 2:14–16

- *Rom* 1:20–21

Recommended *Catechism* References

- CCC 1776-1778
- CCC 1780-1782
- CCC 1783-1785

Vocabulary

Conscience—the interior voice of a human being where his actions are guided by the law of God

Moral Conscience—man's ability to perform good acts and avoid evil ones.

Chapter

Virtue vs. Vice

"Whatever is true, whatever is honorable, whatever is just, whatever is pure, whatever is lovely, whatever is gracious, if there is any excellence, if there is anything worthy of praise, think about these things." —*Phil 4:8*

General Theme

Screwtape classifies the causes of human laughter under four categories; Joy, Fun, the Joke Proper, and Flippancy. The main theme in this chapter reflects distorted definitions of fun and joy, for example. For Screwtape, laughter in relation to joy for God is the worst kind. **The crux here is the desire to have the "patient" act in ways contrary to virtuous behavior, whether it be lustfully, sarcastically, etc. The desire is for direct indecent behavior.** Screwtape defines this whole mission in the following sentence: Cruelty is shameful—unless the cruel man can represent it as a practical joke (Lewis 1942, 55).

And here lies the punch line, convince man that his indecent actions are not indecent.

Debunking Screwtape

Actions or words do not need a negative foundation to foster joy. This is a misrepresentation of what true joy is. The virtue of joy resonates with the love of Christ at its center. Perception is merely perception until you find the truth of the matter. Genuine truth reveals what is real, i.e. good acts vs. bad ones.

Application of the Catechism

The Cardinal virtues, in particular Prudence, provide a gauge to determine virtue from vice. Prudence provides practical reason. In other words, it leads us to choose the good that will lead to further grace. In essence the practice of prudence reveals how good acts result in good outcomes and bad acts into bad outcomes (CCC 1806).

Recommended Scripture References:

- *Phil* 4:8
- *Wisdom* 8:7

Recommended Catechism References:

- CCC 1806
- CCC 1803–1804
- CCC 1788

Vocabulary

Prudence—utilizing practical reason to discern good acts in everyday life.

Virtue—a habitual act to do good.

Chapter **12**

The Great Deception

"If we say we have no sin, we deceive ourselves,
and the truth is not in us." —*1 Jn* 1:8

General Theme

One of the greatest weapons against man's relationship with Christ is the notion that they have done just enough prayer or devotion to "get by." Screwtape encourages Wormwood to have the "patient" continue to attend Church but in reality have no foundation as to why he still practices his Christian faith. **"As long as he retains externally the habits of a Christian he can still be made to think of himself as one who has adopted a few new friends and amusements but whose spiritual state is much the same as it was six weeks ago"** (Lewis 1942, 58). This particular sentiment serves as the main theme in this chapter. The exterior represents the perception of fidelity, while interiorly, the complete opposite is present, hence the Great Deception.

Debunking Screwtape

St. Paul reminds us of our own penchant for fooling ourselves: Let no one deceive himself. If anyone among you thinks that he is wise in this age, let him become a fool that he may become wise. For the wisdom of this world is folly with God. For it is written, 'He catches the wise in their craftiness,'" (*1 Cor* 3:18–19).

Though the act of deception is intimately associated with sin, at its core it cannot destroy moral truth. Why? The soul of man serves as the source of good and evil acts, given by God himself. What Screwtape describes as the uneasiness of the "patient" is the experiencing of the battle between good and evil. Repentance is always right around the corner. This is why Screwtape encourages Wormwood to keep this person "in the dark", so to speak.

Application of the *Catechism*

A general definition of sin in continuity with the *Catechism* is: an act that encourages concupiscence. Sin presents a false attraction to act in accord with a distorted desire (CCC 1869).

- Concupiscence is at the heart of deception other than the act of sin itself.

- Jesus reminds us that his mercy is limitless.

- Regardless of the habit a person dives into, e.g. distractions while praying, seeking alternatives to Christ's love, e.g. a newspaper, a colleague and so on.

- The *Catechism* reminds us; anyone who deliberately refuses to accept his mercy by repenting rejects the forgiveness of sins and the salvation offered by the Holy Spirit (CCC 1864).

- The act of deception initially convinces the person there is no need for mercy. The greater need is satisfying those pleasures that appear more enjoyable than Christ and His Church.

Recommended Scripture References:

- *Mt* 12:31
- *Lk* 12:10
- *1 Cor* 3:18–19
- *1 Jn* 1:18
- *Rev* 19:20
- *Rev* 20:10

Recommended *Catechism* References:

- CCC 1864
- CCC 1865
- CCC 1868
- CCC 1849–1850

Vocabulary

Vice—an acquired habit that leads to habitual sin

Sin—an offense against God. It is also an offense against truth, reason, justice etc.

Chapter **13**

Truth, Beauty, Goodness

"The truth that enlightens every man was coming into the world." —*Jn* 1:9

General Theme

There is a fear the "patient" will experience the gift of grace through repentance. Screwtape scolds Wormwood for allowing the "patient" to enjoy a good book that he relates to his friends. The fear is allowing the "patient" to experience positive pleasures, or in other words, truth, beauty, and goodness.

Debunking Screwtape

The realization with authentic pleasure is its authentic character. True pleasure has a Christocentric foundation. In Christ the love of God is revealed by the very nature of God's only-begotten Son coming into the world. Self-abandonment to natural truth, beauty, and goodness reflects the Divinity of God who is truth par excellence.

Application of the *Catechism*

Man tends by nature toward the truth. He is obliged to honor and bear witness to it (CCC 2467). Man's dignity calls for this action to be practiced. *As a person created in the image and likeness of God we are created to live in truth.*

Goodness has an order in the genesis of the world. God created the universe in an ordered way. The Devil desires a disordered good. This means guiding man to an attachment of the world versus an attachment to Jesus Christ. **"Because creation comes forth from God's goodness; it shares in that goodness . . ."** (CCC 299).

The practice of goodness is accompanied by spontaneous spiritual joy and moral beauty. Likewise truth carries with it the joy and splendor of spiritual beauty. Truth is beautiful in itself.

Truth is:

- Beauty
- Is found in the ordered creation
- Open to the mystery of God
- An Authentic human expression of love
- A work of wisdom
- An Authentic love of the Father to his children (CCC 2500).

Recommended Scripture References:

- *Wis* 11:20

- *Gen* 1:26
- *Jn* 1:9
- *Rom* 9:21
- *Mt* 12:35
- *Heb* 13:16
- *3 Jn* 11

Recommended Catechism References:

- CCC 299
- CCC 2500
- CCC 2467

Vocabulary:

Truth—authentic beauty created by God. Naturally inclined to reveal and speak what is authentic and real.

Beauty—the natural created reality given to us be God in our own creation and that of the world.

Goodness—an act ordered by the creation of God to exhibit charity to others.

Chapter

Humble Thyself!

"Humble yourselves therefore under the mighty hand of God, that in due time he may exalt you."
—*1 Pt 5:6*

General Theme

Humility strikes at the heart of Screwtape. The "patient" has unfortunately developed a sense of humility. Screwtape would rather have the "patient" recognize his humility and act on it under false pretenses than naturally be humble without recognition of his acts. Screwtape wants to make sure man turns his attention to himself rather than God. **The key theme is to conceal the true end of humility.**

Debunking Screwtape

Humility serves as an action of self-abandonment. This means our emphasis is not on our own needs but on what God desires for us. You place yourself before others in a natural, loving way. Thus, understanding your great talents at writing, for example, should serve to stand on its own without further acclamation or desire for more recognition. The virtue of Humility recognizes God as the author of everything good. At the heart of men rests the knowledge that we are nothing without God. Pride attempts to sway our thinking from God to ourselves.

Application of the *Catechism*

The *Catechism* reminds us of our call to have a poverty of heart. This means our preference should be to Christ first before anything else. Luke reminds the Apostles about the cost of discipleship and their call to renounce everything they have for Christ (*Lk* 14:33).

"All Christ's faithful are to direct their affections rightly lest they be hindered in their pursuit of perfect charity by the use of worldly things and by an adherence to riches which is contrary to the spirit of evangelical poverty" (CCC 2345). We are called to be poor in spirit, recognizing the awesome power of God and His goodness revealed through His son Jesus Christ. In a practical way, our call is to live the beatitudes, i.e. poor in spirit (*Mt* 5:3).

> "The world speaks of voluntary humility as
> poverty in spirit; the Apostle gives an example
> of God's poverty when he says; for your sakes
> he became poor."   —St. Gregory of Nyssa

Recommended Scripture Passages:

- *Lk* 14:33

- *Lk* 21:4

- *Mt* 5:3

Recommended *Catechism* References:

- CCC 2544–2547

- CCC 1716

Vocabulary

Humility—the call of all Catholics to acknowledge God as the author of all good. An avoidance of pride. Humility serves as the foundation for our prayer to God.

Poverty of Spirit—voluntary humility.

Chapter 15

Heaven or?

"If you then have been raised with Christ, seek
things that are above, where Christ is, seated at
the right hand of God. Set you minds on things
that are above, not on things that are on earth.

—*Col* 3:1–3

General Theme

The classic good versus evil battle line is exhibited with Screwtapes' desire to lead man away from a desire for Heaven through a preparation on earth. "**The humans live in time but our Enemy destines them to eternity. He therefore, I believe, wants them to attend chiefly to two things, to eternity itself, and to that point of time which they call the Present**" (Lewis 1942, 75).

Another aspect to look at is the desire to have man dwell on the past (despair) and to look at the future without a firm foundation in Christ. The future is seen as a replacement for Heaven. Man will tend to concentrate on what he can do instead of preparing himself for Heaven. "Hence nearly all vices are rooted in the future" (Lewis 1942, 76).

Debunking Screwtape

Screwtape knows that the creation of the world by God is an ordered good. Earth serves as the proving ground for man's relationship with the Blessed Trinity to flourish. The aim for all of God's children is eternal rest in Heaven. Our responsibility as children of God is to prepare ourselves for God's love. The Church on earth represents the Heavenly kingdom realized through the Holy Sacrifice of the Mass. It is a foretaste of what is to come.

Application of the *Catechism*

The world was created for the sake of the Church. God created the world for the sake of communion with His divine life, a communion brought about by the "convocation" of men in Christ, and this "convocation" is the Church (CCC 760).

> The Church is the goal of all things, and God permitted such painful upheavals as the angels' fall and man's sin only as occasions and means for displaying all the power and his arm and the whole measure of the love he wanted to give the world   —(CCC 760).

Recommended Scripture References:

- *Col* 3:1–3

- *Acts* 10:55
- *Jn* 10:1–21

Recommended *Catechism* References:

- CCC 759
- CCC 760-766

Vocabulary

People of God—the Church, the people who make up the body of Christ.

Chapter **16**

❡ Church of Convenience

*"For he has made known to us in all wisdom and
insight into the mystery of his will, according to
his purpose which he set forth in Christ as a plan
for the fullness of time, to unite all things in him,
things in heaven and things on earth."*

—*Eph* 1:9–10

General Theme

As a matter of convenience, Screwtape encourages
"Wormwood to discourage the "patient" from attending one
particular church. Instead, he should be acquainted with
various churches. **Why? To prevent him from receiving
and embracing a genuine desire for God through the sermon, Church environment etc. Strengthening this notion
is Screwtape's encouragement to find the least faithful and
innocuous Church environment sure to foster endless bore-
dom.** An example is the following: At the other church we
have Fr. Spike. The humans are often puzzled to understand

the range of his opinions; why he is "one day almost a Communist and the next not far from some kind of theocratic Fascism-one day a scholastic, and the next prepared to deny human reason altogether . . ." (Lewis 1942, 83).

Debunking Screwtape

The Church serves as the wellspring of grace. Its source is the Blessed Trinity and its foundation is rooted in the Word made flesh. Regardless of the personal disposition of the priest, the holy sacrifice of the Mass is firmly rooted in the Incarnation. The Church serves as a conversion of heart. This is what Screwtape fears the most. Active engagement in the Mass is the enemy's greatest fear.

Application of the *Catechism*

The Church serves to help the laity exercise (share) their role as priest, prophet and king. By our baptism we are called to participate in this mission that we have been entrusted with by God through His Church (CCC 871). We are called to build up the body of Christ. By virtue of our Baptism, our participation in the mysteries of Christ, i.e. the Mass, leads us to a firm foundation of faith in Him (CCC 872-873).

The vocation of the laity calls us to:

- Engage in the temporal affairs (visible-tangible) and direct them to the will of God.

- Illuminate these acts to further the Kingdom.

- Proclaim the Gospel.

- Incorporate Christ into the stream of society.
- Spread the word of Salvation to all (CCC 898–890).

Recommended Scripture References:

- *Eph* 1:9–10
- *Rom* 8:9
- *Acts* 20:28–29

Recommended *Catechism* References:

- CCC 872–873
- CCC 898–890

Vocabulary

Vocation—a genuine discernment and calling to follow the will of God to attain perfect holiness in Heaven.

Laity—non-ordained faithful individuals who are part of the body of Christ. Incorporated into the Church by Baptism, we are made part of the People of God.

17

Self-Mastery

*"The man said, 'The woman whom you gave to be
with me, she gave me fruit of the tree and I ate.'
Then the Lord God said to the woman, 'What is
this that you have done?' The woman said, 'The
serpent beguiled me, and I ate.' "*

—Gen 3:12–13

General Theme

We have two distinct actions occurring here. First,
Screwtape is reflecting on the actions of the "patient's" mother
and her gluttonous ways. The patent theme with the mothers'
actions is her interior motive. Though externally she appears
to be content with what she receives, internally her desire to
have everything only the way she likes it is stronger. Her freedom is skewed due to her material desires.

The son on the other hand is tempted not with a desire of
gluttony, but a desire regarding chastity. Man is not tempted
with actions related to food; his greatest temptation rests with

chastity. Thus sexual immorality becomes the driving force for Screwtape towards the "patient."

Debunking Screwtape

Man, ultimately has freedom to choose. The Devil, in this case Wormwood, can only propose gluttony or impurity. At their core, man's actions will or will not engage in sinful behavior. Reason and will are two qualities man possesses. Humanity rests on these two principle characteristics because of their nature rooted in the soul and driven by grace.

Application of the *Catechism*

The *Catechism* reminds us man's actions are open to good or evil if he has not bound himself to the ultimate good which is God (CCC 1732). Thus, the possibility of evil acts exists, spurring a continuous battle between good and evil. Good acts foster a genuine freedom not enslaved by sinful acts that destroy the soul.

Authentic freedom holds man accountable for his acts. The goal for all humanity is a visible progression toward the good, i.e. God. Self-mastery of one's actions reflect a desire to respect oneself, others and God (CCC 2339). In the area of sexual morality, chastity defines self-mastery and true freedom of sexual pleasures (*Sir* 1:22). The virtue of temperance engages moderation of attractive pleasures (CCC 1809; *1 Jn* 3:3).

Recommended Scripture References:

- *1 Jn* 3:3

- *Gen* 3:12–13
- *Sir* 1:22
- *Titus* 2:1–6

Recommended *Catechism* References:

- CCC 2338–2342
- CCC 1809
- CCC 1732

Vocabulary

Temperance—moderation in attractive pleasures

Chastity—successful integration of sexuality within a human being between one man and woman as a life-long mutual gift (Marriage).

Chapter

18

Sex, a Gift from God

"For this is the will of God, your sanctification:
that you abstain from immorality; that each one of
you knows how to control his own body in holiness
and honor, not in the passion of lust like heathens
who do not know God. . . For God has not called
us for uncleanness, but in holiness. Therefore who-
ever disregards this, disregards not man but God,
who gives his Holy Spirit to you."

—*1 Thess 4:3–8*

General Theme

Screwtape in a way is exasperated with the "enemy's" philosophy on sex. **He views love as impossible when dealing with human lustful desires. Humans should use one another for mere pleasure.** The notion of love is an afterthought. He detests monogamy. "The enemy's demand on humans takes the form of a dilemma; either complete abstinence or unmitigated monogamy. Screwtape mocks the "enemies" of one flesh regarding marriage between one man and one woman. In a straightforward way, Screwtape prefers infidelity and all it has to offer.

Debunking Screwtape

All God's children desire love. This is the essence of the soul. Love your neighbor as yourself (*Mt* 22:34-40). Humanity is called to love. The soul calls for such an act because of God's love for His children. Love within the proper bonds of holy matrimony is indissoluble. The union between man and woman in matrimony cannot be broken. The two greatest gifts of marriage are love of spouse and love of children. Chastity within marriage is a gift, expressed through the free sexual intimacy of husband and wife.

Application of the *Catechism*

Conjugal love requires the fidelity of spouses (CCC 1646). Love is definitive (CCC 1646). The foundation of conjugal love is rooted in fidelity to God, to His covenant and to His Church. Fidelity rests on authentic conjugal love. The issue of either unmitigated monogamy or abstinence is not an impediment towards true love as viewed by Screwtape.

> "Sexuality affects all aspects of the human person in the unity of his body and soul. It especially concerns affectivity, the capacity to love and to procreate, and in a more general way the aptitude for forming bonds of communion with others"   —(CCC 2332).

Recommended Scripture References:

- *Mt* 5:27–28
- *1 Thess* 4:3–8
- *Eph* 5:21
- *Gal* 6:2

Recommended Scripture References:

- CCC 1643
- CCC 1646
- CCC 2331
- CCC 2332–2335

Vocabulary

Conjugal love—free consent of spouses in fidelity toward one another in the act of love.

Fidelity—faithfulness toward God and His Church. Also reflects faithfulness of spouses to one another.

Chapter

Understanding Divine Love

> *"His divine power has granted to us all things*
> *that pertain to life and godliness, through the*
> *knowledge of him who called us to his own glory*
> *and excellence, by which he has granted to us his*
> *precious and very great promises that through*
> *these you may escape from the corruption that is*
> *in the world because of passion, and become par-*
> *takers of the divine nature."* —2 Pet 1:4

General Theme

It is not possible that God can love creatures that are not like him, or so Screwtape thinks. God is God; man is not. **God's love of man is a "disguise" (Lewis 1942, 100). He views this sort of love as a nuisance. What can God have to gain from this outpouring of love to man? Another aspect Screwtape brings up is the background behind the Devil's ouster from Heaven.** He mentions that the Devil himself questioned God's intent of creating man even though a cross was foreseen on man (Lewis 1942, 100). God would not tell the Devil why. This secret which is true love, that is sacrifice, the Devil could not understand even if presented clearly.

Debunking Screwtape

"For God so loved the world, that He gave His only-begotten Son, that whoever believes in Him should not perish but have eternal life" (*Jn* 3:15-16). Screwtape's inability to understand true love is his greatest downfall and that of his father the Devil. The word became flesh to know God's love through His son Jesus Christ (CCC 456).

Application of the *Catechism*

God desires to communicate His divine life to the men he freely created (CCC 52). This means He desires to show us His grace and mercy. God's intent is to give us grace in preparation for our journey to Heaven. He wants our response to His revelation of love. God's love is fully revealed through His son, the Word made flesh, in order to partake of His divine nature. The Son of God became man so that we might become sons and daughters of God (CCC 460). The epitome of God's love, so to speak, rested on His son's death on the cross, while we still rejected him.

Keep in mind, the virtue of charity calls us to love God above all things not for our own sake but primarily for His own. This virtue also calls us to love our neighbor as ourselves (CCC 1822).

Recommended Scripture References:

- *Jn* 3:15–16
- *2 Pet* 1:4
- *Eph* 1:9
- *1 Tim* 6:16

Recommended Scripture References:

- CCC 51–52
- CCC 456; 460
- CCC 1602
- CCC 1825–1826

Vocabulary

Charity—to love God above all things; love of neighbor as yourself.

Revelation of God—God's desire to reveal and make known the mystery of His will.

Chapter

20

Sexual Integrity

"You have heard that it was said, 'You shall not commit adultery'." —Mt 5:27

General Theme

Successful sexual integration is an anomaly for Screwtape and Wormwood. The essence of this chapter is to encourage the "patient" to use his gift of sexuality as a means to misdirect it in an improper form. The methods of this improper form originate in the exploitation of human sexuality through advertisements, art, television etc. Another attempt is to dissuade sexuality within marriage and encourage sex outside of the covenant of marriage. Still another method is to pervert sex by emphasizing its physical aspects above its interior aspect, which is the genuine love of the spouses.

Debunking Screwtape

By our baptism we are called to chastity. The first sacrament of initiation imprints an indelible mark on our soul as children of God. We become immersed in His love (*Gal* 3:27). Screwtape can't undo a permanent seal given by Christ to all. Human beings have the capacity of self-mastery when it comes to sex. Freedom works both ways, for good and bad actions.

Application of the *Catechism*

The following catechetical guidelines provide us with a blue-print of exercising authentic freedom and self-mastery.

Whoever wants to remain faithful to his baptismal promises and resist temptations will want to adopt the means for doing so:

- Self-Knowledge
- Practice of an Ascesis adapted to the situations that confront him
- Obedience to God's Commandments
- Exercise of the Moral Virtues (Prudence, Temperance, Fortitude, Justice)
- Fidelity to Prayer, i.e. the "Our Father" (CCC 2340).

St. Ambrose provides us with three forms of Chastity, no one greater than the other (CCC 2349).

1. Spouses.
2. Widows
3. Virgins

Sexuality is ordered to:

- The conjugal love of man and woman.

- The married state; the physical intimacy of spouses becomes a sign and pledge of spiritual communion.

- Sanctification via Baptism.

- A proper action of love man and woman committed to each other.

- The innermost being of each human person (CCC 2360-2361).

Recommended Scripture References:

- *Gal* 3:27

- *Mt* 5:27

- *Gen* 4:1–2

- *Titus* 2:1–6

Recommended Catechism References:

- CCC 2340–2344

- CCC 2360–2361

- CCC 2348

Vocabulary

Temperance—moderating the attraction of pleasures

Chastity—successful sexual integration within the person. Leads to respect for the dignity of the human person.

Chapter **21**

A Clouded Intellect

"Are you still without understanding?"

—*Mt* 15:16

General Theme

If you cloud man's intellect, then his view of the world becomes egocentric. This means man develops a mindset where the world is supposed to revolve around him. Time is defined by how he sees it in his life. Screwtape tells Wormwood "the sense of ownership is always to be encouraged. The humans are always putting up claims of ownership which sound equally funny in Heaven and in Hell and we must keep them doing so" (Lewis 1942, 113). **The central theme of this chapter is to convince man he is the supreme master of his body and thus can do what he pleases with it without interruption.**

Debunking Screwtape

Though man can in theory think he is the reason for his own existence, the reality is that mankind reflects the love of only one creator. God is the author of life. He gave man his identity which reflects His own. The Devil knows this hence the constant attempt to cloud man's intellect from seeing reality.

Application of the *Catechism*

Can man live with bread alone (*Mt* 4:4)? Man's creation rests on God. God creates man out of his own free will. He desires us to share in his love (CCC 295). A summary of what God does for man is as follows:

To human beings God even;

- Gives the power to freely share in His providence by entrusting them with the responsibility of 'subduing' the earth and having dominion over it.

- Enables man to be intelligent and free causes in order to complete the work of creation

- Allows perfection of harmony for their own good and that of neighbors.

- Allows man to enter deliberately into the divine plan by their actions, their prayers, and their sufferings (CCC 307, See: *Col* 1:24).

Recommended Scripture References:

- *1 Cor* 3:9

- *Col* 4:11
- *Mt* 4:4
- *Mt* 15:16

Recommended *Catechism* References:

- CCC 306–307
- CCC 295–296

Vocabulary

Creation—God giving a beginning to all around him. He is the author of life.

Chapter **22**

Witness

"He came for testimony, to bear witness to the light . . ."   —*Jn* 1:7

General Theme

The "patient" is in love with, of all things, a practicing Christian. For Screwtape and Wormwood, this is the worst type. Faithful belief in God and His Church are the worst qualities this particular girl has. Screwtape calls here a "little cheat" for having such a profound faith and influence over the "patient" and his relationship with God.

Debunking Screwtape

Authentic conversion is spurred by authentic witness. Witnessing the faith exudes truth, beauty, and goodness. All of God's children are called to bear witness to the truth (*Acts* 10:41).

Application of the *Catechism*

The laity fulfills their prophetic mission by evangelization through the proclamation of Christ by word and testimony (CCC 905; 908; 910).

Recommended Scripture References:

- *Jn* 1:17
- *Acts* 10:41
- *Jn* 21:24
- *Acts* 10:43

Recommended *Catechism* References:

- CCC 905; 908
- CCC 897; 904
- CCC 942

Vocabulary

Evangelization—proclamation of the Gospel—teach, preach, catechize from the Word of God.

23

The Corrupted Mind
and the Historical Jesus

*"But when the time had fully come, God sent
forth his Son, born of a woman, born under the
law, to redeem those who were under the law, so
that we might receive adoption as sons."*

—*Gal* 4:4–5

General Theme

The way to corrupt the mind of the Christian is to corrupt their view of Christ. Screwtape instructs Wormwood
to attack the heart of all believers. If they can convince the
"patient" Christ is a mere historical figure among other significant historical figures, then the notion of Christ as the Son of
God Redeemer of the World takes a lesser significance in the
heart and mind of all believers. All this is predicated by the
influence of the family of the "patients" girlfriend so to speak

who are devout Christians. The main theme here is discredited Christ as a mere historical figure.

Debunking Screwtape

History reveals Jesus Christ is more than historical. He is a living reality made present through His Sacrifice on the Cross as the Son of God, the second person of the Blessed Trinity. Merely looking at Jesus as a historical figure is to dismiss the saving reality that continues today through the visible one, holy, Catholic and apostolic Church. In essence, this particular historical notion strips the source and summit of the Christian life, i.e. the Holy Eucharist. The Holy Eucharist above anything else represents the continual saving reality truly present in the form of bread and wine.

Application of the *Catechism*

The following article from the *Catechism* reveals more than a historical fact:

We believe and confess that Jesus of Nazareth, born a Jew of a daughter of Israel at Bethlehem at the time of King Herod the Great and the emperor Caesar Augustus, a carpenter by trade who died crucified in Jerusalem under Pontius Pilate during the reign of Tiberius, is the eternal Son of God made man. He came from God, descended from heaven and came in the flesh" (CCC 423).

At the heart of all catechetical instruction is in essence the person of Jesus Christ (CCC 426). This particular point is important in refuting the Historical Jesus concept. Jesus represents the very presence of God. If Jesus is a historical figure of the past, then God falls into the same thought. As the only-begotten Son of God, Jesus holds the unique characteristic as fully human and fully divine (CCC 442; 464; 470).

Keep in mind that the Word became flesh:

- In order to save us by reconciling us with God (CCC 457).
- So that we might know God's love (CCC 458).
- To be our model of holiness (CCC 459).
- To make us partakers of the Divine nature (CCC 460).

Recommended Scripture References:

- *1 Jn* 1:1–4
- *1 Jn* 4:10
- *Jn* 3:16
- *Jn* 13:3
- *Jn* 3:13
- *Rom* 10:6–13
- *Acts* 4:12

Recommended Catechism References:

- CCC 423–426
- CCC 430–433

- CCC 436; 440; 442
- CCC 457–460

Vocabulary

Jesus—the second person of the Blessed Trinity, the only-begotten Son of God, was crucified on the cross to ransom the souls of humanity.

Incarnation—the word of God takes on human form in the person of Jesus Christ. The Son of God assumed human form.

Holy Eucharist—the principal Christian liturgical celebration centered on the consecration of bread and wine by a priest into the actual body of blood of Christ. It is one of the seven sacraments of the Church is part of the sacraments of initiation.

Mediator—Jesus Christ the Son of God is the mediator between God and humanity.

Chapter  24

Dignity of the Human Person

"Blessed are the pure of Heart, for they shall see God."   —Mt 5:3–12

General Theme

You are who you associate with. If this statement were completely true, we would carefully gauge our friends. The issue of pride and the lack of respect are the weapons of choice for Screwtape and Wormwood toward the "patient" and the patient's "young woman." **The aim here is to convince the "patient" he is not worthy of the "young woman" because of his demeanor and the new intellectual friends the "patient" has chosen to associate with. Screwtape tells us: Success here depends on confusing the patient** (Lewis 1942, 132).

Debunking Screwtape

Screwtape's attempt to confuse the "patient" fails in not understanding the ability of human beings altogether. The

Beatitudes are an integral part of human action. They respond to the natural desire for happiness (CCC 1718). True happiness has its origin in God. God has placed this gift in the heart of all mankind. Screwtape's attempt to draw a negative outlook from the "patient" to the "young woman" fails to understand the dignity each possesses.

Application of the *Catechism*

God calls man to echo the following beatitudes:

- Prepare for the coming of the Kingdom of God.

- The vision of God.

- Enter into the joy of the Lord.

- Enter into God's rest (CCC 1720).

The Gift of Justification tells us:

- We take part in Christ's Passion by dying to sin.

- We take part in his Resurrection by being born to a new life via Baptism.

- We are members of His body which is the Church.

We can do nothing without God's love. This means His gift of grace is something to embrace and apply. Grace calls us to become children of God. Grace will help the "patient" see the value of the "young woman" as a child of God and not as a nuisance. Grace allows us to participate in the life of God.

Recommended Scripture References:

- *Jn* 1:12–8
- *Mt* 5:3–12
- *Jn* 15:1–4

Recommended *Catechism* References:

- CCC 1718–1720
- CCC 1987–1997

Vocabulary

Grace—a free gift from God given to us via the Holy Spirit to participate in God's life.

Beatitude—the teachings of Jesus on the Sermon on the Mount (See *Mt* 5:3-12).

Chapter

25

Putting on a False Face

"Beware of the false prophets, who come to you in sheep's clothing, but inwardly are ravenous wolves." —Mt 7:15

General Theme

The thought of relativity by itself may appear harmless. We human beings tend to compare things at almost every turn. In many ways we have an insatiable appetite to find something better. This is where the term "everything is relative" can take on greater meaning. Screwtape makes the argument that he is willing to concede a practicing Christian so as long as he couples the practicing Christian characteristic with another characteristic aimed to reduce the fervent practice of Christianity. **"If they must be Christians let them at least be Christians with a difference. Substitute for the faith itself some Fashion with a Christian colouring. Work on their horror of the same Old Thing"** (Lewis 1942, 135).

Hence, the notion "everything is relative" takes a unique turn based on Screwtape's intent to relativize Christianity with something else. In other words, bring Christianity to the point where you see no difference in practicing the faith as compared to watching television. This point is echoed further where Screwtape views liturgical participation as an opportunity to foster a complacent attitude where the Mass is seen as novelty.

Debunking Screwtape

Though the practice of the Liturgical year for Catholics may seem redundant, the intent of the liturgical cycles (x3) is to draw a continual and deeper awareness of the love Christ has for us. The Liturgy does stand on its own merit. The Sacrifice of the Mass will forever draws us into an intimacy that is not matched from a prior one. Meaning, every time we engage our faith, especially in the Mass, we are drawn ever closer to Him.

Application of the *Catechism*

The *Catechism* has a direct response for eliminating novelty in relation to our faith. The Church's Magisterium exercises the authority it holds from Christ to the fullest extent when it defines dogmas, that is, when it;

- proposes, in a form obliging the Christian people to an irrevocable adherence of faith,

- defines truths contained in divine Revelation

- or also when it proposes, in a definitive way, truths having a necessary connection with these.

Our spiritual life is connected to doctrine (CCC 89). This means if both are in tandem, the notion of the Church being a novelty will be far less reaching. Another important point to realize is that everything within the Church is connected. The "Analogy of Faith" means that all the truths of the Church are interrelated because at its heart is the revelation of God's plan.

Faith seeks understanding, not complacency. At the heart of man is a desire to come to the knowledge of truth (CCC 158, *See also* CCC 1153–1158).

> "The grace of faith opens the desires of the Heart."   —*Eph* 1:18

> "I believe in order to understand; and I understand, the better to believe."
> —St. Augustine, Sermon 43, 7, 9: PL 38, 257–258

Recommended Scripture References:

- *Jn* 8:31–32
- *Mt* 7:15
- *Rom* 12:6
- *Eph* 1:18

Recommended *Catechism* References:

- CCC 88–89

- CCC 110–113
- CCC 158
- CCC 95
- CCC 1153–1158

Vocabulary

Creed—a profession of the Christian faith e.g. Apostles Creed; Nicene Creed

Doctrine/Dogma—the teachings of Jesus Christ proclaimed by the Church Magisterium / The faithful are obliged to believe in the truths of the faith.

Chapter **26**

Moral Ambiguity

"Bear one another's burdens, and so fulfill the law of Christ." —*Gal* 6:2

General Theme

Screwtape goes after the foundation of humanity; the Sacrament of Holy Matrimony. **The notion of unsatisfied desires is one element Screwtape preaches against the love of spouses. Another is convincing husband and wife they are truly selfless in their actions toward one another when in reality they are not.**

"You must make them establish as a Law for their whole married life that degree of mutual self-sacrifice which is at present sprouting naturally out of the enchantment, but which, when the enchantment dies away, they will not have charity enough to enable them to perform. They will not see the trap, since they are under the double blindness of mistaking sexual excitement for charity and of thinking that the excitement will last" (Lewis 1942, 142–143).

The emphasis here is to create a marital ambiguity at the heart of the marital covenant, i.e. the conjugal, fruitful, charitable love of each spouse. In other words, Screwtape creates false charity.

Debunking Screwtape

Even if Screwtape and Wormwood were successful in twisting the outlook of each spouse into a perversion of sorts, the covenantal bond between them is still formed in Christ at the heart. We are called to keep God's law out of love. This love reflects the active practice of a moral life towards each spouse.

True conjugal love involves a totality, in which all the elements of the person enter:

- Appeal of the body

- Instinct

- Power of feeling

- Affectivity

- Aspiration of the spirit and of will

It aims at:

- A deep personal unity

- forming one heart and soul

- indissolubility and faithfulness in definitive mutual giving (CCC 1643).

Application of the *Catechism*

True love of spouses requires indissolubility towards one another. Once joined in the bonds of Holy Matrimony, both are no longer two but one. Screwtape attempts to manipulate this couple rest on not having indissolubility present between both spouses. Each spouse is called to grow daily in communion by mutually giving him(her) self to the other. This human communion is completed by communion in Jesus Christ through the sacrament of holy matrimony (CCC 1644).

Characteristics of Conjugal Love:

- Fidelity of spouses, i.e. faithfulness to one another

- It is definitive.

- It is not an arrangement.

- It respects the Dignity of the human person (CCC 1780).

- It is driven by the moral good.

- It assumes proper responsibility toward the other.

- It is centered on God Himself (CCC 1646–1648).

Recommended Scripture References

- *Gal* 6:2

- *Gal* 5:22

- *1 Cor* 13:13

- *Eph* 5:21

- *Gen* 2:24

- *Mk* 10:9
- *Mt* 19:1–12

Recommended *Catechism* References

- CCC 1643–1644
- CCC 1646–1648
- CCC 1780
- CCC 2360–2365

Vocabulary

Charity—the theological virtue of love.

Conscience—the inner voice of the human being guided by the law of God to make right choices and avoid evil ones.

Covenant—a solemn agreement between human being(s) or between a human being and God. In the case of the Sacrament of Holy Matrimony, man and woman come together in the sacrament of Holy Matrimony to form a bond with God and each other.

Chapter

27

False Spirituality

"And when you pray, you must not be like the
hypocrites; for they love to stand and pray in the
synagogues and at the street corners, that they
may be seen by men." —Mt 6:5

General Theme

Wormwood is directed to encourage a false spiritual-
ity on the "patient." Praise should be encouraged every time
the "patient" or anyone prays for that matter. Another point
is presenting the notion that intercessory prayer is useless if
the petition is not answered. Encouraging disobedience from
prayer if the prayer is not answered serves as a weapon for
Wormwood and Screwtape. **Ignorance of the Divine reality,**
God in relation to prayer, is part of the plan. In summary, why
bother to pray if nothing really happens.

Debunking Screwtape

Prayer is not erroneous. It is communication with God.

God is always communicating with us. Screwtape knows this but does not fully grasp why there is constant communication between both. This is why Jesus gave us the "Our Father" (*Mt* 6:7–15). Prayer can be difficult. Some examples of these difficulties are:

- Distraction—habitual difficulty to pray

- Dryness—when your heart is separated from God when trying to pray

- Lack of faith—most common form where there is a lack of love.

- Acedia—carelessness in prayer, decreased vigilance or discipline in prayer (CCC 2729-2733).

These difficulties are overcome through perseverance in prayer. Man can overcome these challenges.

Application of the *Catechism*

There is no other way of Christian Prayer than Christ. Whether personal, communal, vocal, or interior, we have access to the Father when we pray (CCC 2664).

The name Jesus is the name above any other name when we pray. The prayer of the Church driven by the Word of God in the celebration of the Liturgy teaches us to pray to the Lord Jesus (CCC 2665).

> "For me, prayer is a surge of the heart; it is a simple look turned toward heaven, it is a cry of recognition and of love, embracing both trial and joy."　　　　　—St. Thérèse of Lisieux

There are several forms of prayer:

- Blessing—the basic movement of Christian Prayer

- Adoration—acknowledging God as above all things

- Petition—calling upon our awareness of God in prayer for others. Petition means to turn back to God.

- Intercession—prayer of petition leading us to pray as Jesus prays.

- Thanksgiving—offering of thanksgiving centered on the sacrifice of the Mass

- Praise—form of prayer which recognizes most immediately that God is God (CCC 2626-2643).

Ultimate Prayer

The Holy Eucharist is the complete and most pure form of prayer. It offers the body of Christ in its entirety, pure and undefiled in the glory of God's name. It is the true sacrifice of praise (CCC 2643, 1330).

The Lord's Prayer

The Lord's Prayer serves as the perfect prayer as it communicates God's plan for humanity. In other words, it is a communication of His love throughout all of history. This is the only prayer given to us directly by Christ Himself to and through the Apostles. It is the prayer of the Church prayed by the Apostles and the early disciples (CCC 2762-2766).

It is a liturgical prayer since its place is firmly within the liturgy and the sacraments (CCC 2768-2769).

Recommended Scripture Passages:

- *Lk* 24:44
- *Jn* 17:7
- *Mt* 6:7–15
- *Eph* 6:18
- *Jn* 15:5
- *1 Pet* 1:3–9
- *Lk* 18:13
- *1 Jn* 3:22
- *Ps* 130:1
- *Lk* 18:9–14

Recommended Catechism References:

- CCC 2559
- CCC 2607–2608
- CCC 2616
- CCC 2626–2643
- CCC 2762–2766
- CCC 2700–2719
- CCC 2725–2734
- CCC 2759–2772

Vocabulary: See lesson plan above.

28

Preparing for Heaven or Earth

"For to me to live is Christ, and to die is gain."
—*Phil* 1:21

General Theme

Death eventually comes to us all. We do not know the hour or the day. Historically, mankind has exhibited a fear of death. **Death was brought to a clearer understanding through the death and resurrection of Christ. His Crucifixion provided the foundation man can hold on to in preparation for our final resting place in Heaven if we choose this path.**

Screwtape instructs Wormwood to encourage man's desire for an earthly life versus a heavenly one. The aim is to embrace what is on earth and not what is to come in heaven.

Debunking Screwtape

Man has already prepared for death via Baptism. The first sacrament of initiation prepares us to die in Christ's grace

(CCC 1010). St. Paul reminds us of his desire to depart from the earth and be with Christ (*Phil* 1:23). All of God's children are created for the sole purpose of being called by God to Himself.

Application of the *Catechism*

Earth is temporary for mankind. Heaven is our true eternal home. Thus, we are called to die in God's grace and live a life of purity for the sake of the Kingdom. Our life is meant to be a Trinitarian one, of Father, Son, and Holy Spirit. The sign of the Cross serves as the distinctive marker of our Christian life and our desire for our final rest in Heaven (CCC 1023-1024).

Heaven is our final end, our communion with the Blessed Trinity, the Mother of God and all the angels and saints. It is the ultimate end and fulfills our deepest longing (CCC 1024).

Jesus' death and resurrection opened heaven to us (CCC 1026).

Recommended Scripture References:

- *Phil* 1:21
- *Jn* 14:3
- *Rev* 2:17
- *1 Jn* 3:2

Recommended *Catechism* References

- CCC 1024–1025
- CCC 1026
- CCC 1010
- CCC 1028

Vocabulary

Heaven—spending eternal life with God. It is a communion of life and love with the Blessed Trinity.

Chapter **29**

The Character of Hatred

> *"If you keep my commandments, you will abide in my love, just as I have kept my Father's commandments and abide in his love. These things I have spoken to you, that my joy may be in you, and that your joy may be full."* —Jn 15:10–11

General Theme

If at first you don't succeed, tempt him again. Screwtape is determined to have Wormwood tempt the "patient" by any means necessary. The weapon of choice becomes hate. Screwtape directs Wormwood to induce the "patient" into a world view of hate when things go wrong.

Debunking Screwtape

Man, created in the image and likeness of God, brings certain characteristics naturally to the order of creation.

- Man has a soul created by God

- Man is ordered naturally to the good.

- Man is disposed to worship the one true God.

- Man can deviate from his mission (free will and concupiscence).

Screwtape misjudges the ability of man to follow God. He uses the characteristic of a coward to describe him because he fears the virtue of courage which fosters truth.

Application of the *Catechism*

The *Catechism* tells us human virtue is a firm disposition, an attitude that guides our words and actions according to reason and faith (CCC 1804). Virtue diminishes hatred, fear, etc. because our desire in exercising a virtuous life leads to fidelity in right moral action.

A key virtue in this battle is Prudence. As one of the cardinal virtues, Prudence drives practical reason in our every day discernment. Man's conduct is directed in accordance with his application of Prudence (CCC 1806).

Our Christian beatitude is to enter into joy with our Lord (*Mt* 25:21-23).

Recommended Scripture References:

- *Jn* 15:10–11

- *Mt* 25:21–23

- *Wis* 8:7

- *1 Pet* 4:7

Recommended *Catechism* References

- CCC 1804–1806

Vocabulary

Human Virtue—firm disposition or stable attitudes to perform good acts governed by reason and faith.

30

Do You Have Fortitude?

*"The Lord is my strength and my song, he has
become my salvation."* —*Psalm* 118:14

General Theme

When man is at the point of exhaustion, his faculties also
tire, especially his spiritual and emotional well-being. This
is precisely why Screwtape encourages Wormwood to place
more doubt into the "patient's" mind to cause confusion and
more hatred against the world and its Author.

Debunking Screwtape

Man has the ability to exhibit fortitude even through the
most extreme circumstances. As the old saying goes, "God will
never place you in a position you can't handle." Man has the
capacity to suffer and endure hardship without casting blame
on others. Man is created well, and is thus disposed to the
pursuit of good. It is important to note, Jesus has already overcome the world.

Application of the *Catechism*

Fortitude helps us:

- resist temptation
- overcome obstacles in the moral life
- conquer fear of death
- face trials and persecutions.
- be disposed to sacrifice our lives for a just cause (CCC 1808).

Recommended Scripture References:

- *Psalm* 118:14
- *Jn* 16:33

Recommended *Catechism* References:

- CCC 1808; 1804, 2848

Vocabulary

Fortitude—a moral virtue that enables man to be firm in difficult situations, always pursuing the good.

Chapter

31

Deliver Us from Evil

"Deliver us from evil." —Mt 6: 13

General Theme

Screwtape is livid they have lost the "patient." He is especially angry at Wormwood though Screwtape condescendingly tells Wormwood they are closer than before. He is upset on how easily the "patient" slipped through their fingers.

Debunking Screwtape

Jesus Christ has already won. He has fought the good fight and finished His earthly journey through the Paschal Mystery. Screwtape avoids this altogether. Christ's message is too visible and powerful.

Application of the *Catechism*

The last petition of the *Catechism* is to deliver us from the snares and evil of the Devil. Since the battle between good and evil rages on, our primary request should be prayer and help.

The Devil is always there, making him visible. This is the constant battle between good and evil (CCC 2850). Deception versus reality, hope versus despair (CCC 2852).

Our desire is to be free from corruption brought on not only by our actions but also by what the Devil as a pure spirit desires to do further.

Recommended Scripture References

- *1 Jn* 5:18–19
- *Jn* 17:15
- *Jn* 8:44
- *Rev* 12:9

Recommended *Catechism* References

- CCC 2850–2854

Vocabulary

Our Father—the Lord's Prayer that calls on twelve petitions to the Father.

Points on the Catechism Every Catechist Should Know

What the Catechism Emphasizes:

1. The exposition of Doctrine in order to help deepen the understanding of the Catholic faith.

2. A repository of the Deposit of Faith found in Sacred Tradition and Sacred Scripture.

3. A continuity and unity that has never been broken because it is the work of the Divine Teacher Jesus Christ that expresses the content and analogy of faith brought to us by the Divine Teacher himself.

What the Catechism Provides:

1. The need to know and understand the Sacred Deposit of the Faith taught by Our Lord Jesus Christ.

2. A synthesis of Christ's teaching that is preserved through the Bride of Christ, the Church.

3. An exposition of the Faith through an application of Sacred Tradition and Sacred Scripture.

Understanding How to use the Catechism:

1. This Catechism is no mere reference work that we may occasionally consult, like a standard dictionary or encyclopedia.

2. This Catechism is no mere summary of religious ideas or ideals that provide a readable handbook on how Catholics think.

3. No, the Catechism is an indispensable arm of instruction in every level of the teaching apostolate.

Five Recommendations on How to use the Catechism:

1. Know the Catechism by reading it, hearing it, explaining it, meditating on it.

2. Trust the Catechism by knowing it is the truth of the Catholic Church.

3. Adapt the Catechism by adjusting the language to the mentality of those you teach. Adapt ideas without watering them down or confusing their meaning.

4. Live the Catechism by practicing the virtues which Christ expects His followers to do while teaching. God uses good people as channels of grace to others.

5. the Catechism, because in the last day, we shall be judged on our practice of Charity.

Fundamental Tasks of Catechetical Instruction

- To promote the knowledge of the faith (*Heb* 11:1–2).

- To enable the faithful to participate fully. Consciously, and actively in the Liturgical and Sacramental Life (*Jas* 2:1–8).

- To enter into a process of conversion which is evidenced by responses to the social consequences of Gospel imperatives (GDC 87).

- To have all activities be permeated by the spirit of prayer (CT 23).

- To form genuine Christian Communities (GDC 91).

- To educate to a missionary dimension.

Luke 24:28

Catechesis—to make faith "living, conscious and active" through a systematic presentation of the faith, i.e. Deposit of Faith, prayer and witness seeking to bring to maturity the seeds of faith sown by God.

The Call of the Catechist—to echo the word of God (CCC 4)

- *Mt* 28:16–20; CT 13

- Catechesis seeks to make the "faith become alive, conscious and active through the light of instruction (GCD 17).

Essential Tasks of the Catechist

- To promote the knowledge of the faith (Creed) ("I believe in God . . .")

- Liturgical Education (Liturgy and the Sacramental Life)

- Moral Formation (Ten Commandments, Beatitudes, Moral Conscience, Natural Law)-Initiation and Education in community life and mission (GDC 85; CT 4).

A Few Words on Methodology and Content

Catechetical Objective

To assess proper methodology and content as it relates to catechetical instruction within the Classroom.

Points of Emphasis

- An instructor must know the personality of the class and the neediest individuals. (Takes time!)

- Catechesis must be seen as an organic (active participation) education of children into the fullness of the Christian Life.

- Catechesis must not be a "drill" or a "test" but it must be an assessment of the revelation of grace outpoured to the soul of the person.

- Catechesis must be a process of Introduction, Revelation and Initiation.

- Through this process, a relationship with Jesus Christ is formed thus allowing for a proper methodology to be formed.

- Methodology is what the instructor does.

- Learning style is what the student receives.

- Accommodate all learning styles (Visual, Audio, and Kinesthetic)

- Remember: *1 Cor* 11:23 "Through Humility and Discipleship we pass on the "Word." Revelation is what God's word is all about. All, revelation is about Christ Himself."

- Catechesis must be Christo-centric not anthro-centric (man-centered). Catechesis is primarily about God.

St. Augustine's Catechetical Guidelines

St. Augustine's Points to remember

- The Catechist must possess joy in handing on the Deposit of Faith

- The focal point of the catechist's instructions is to know and understand that the chief reason for Christ's coming was to manifest and to teach God's love for us. Here the catechist should find the focal point of his instruction.

- Christ came to manifest the love of the Father for His children.

The Narration

The beginning of any catechetical instruction is to begin with the narration of God's dealings with man from the creation of the world down to the present period of Church History.

- Love is the final cause of their instruction.

- God made all things very good.

The Disposition of the Catechist

- Know your audience
- Catechize with joy.
- *1 Pt* 2:21 – for instructing the ignorant.
- Embrace your audience at their level. Take on the mind of those to be catechized.
- See: *1 Cor* 9:22; *2 Cor* 5:13; *2 Cor* 12:15

Dealing with those in error

- For those who fall in error, we must take care gently and gradually to correct them in a way they can understand.
- Follow the Lord's example when questioned.
- Repeat Instructions.
- Show sympathy, love and compassion to those who do not understand.
- Direct the student to the Love of the Father and the Blessed Trinity.

Does the student understand?

- The catechist must engage the student via questions, and instill confidence in their responses.
- Act in accordance with their answer.

- When someone is bored, switch the approach and the catechetical topic all-together.

- State something in reference to the pupil.

- Offer catechetical distractions to ease the learning environment.

Style of the Discourse

- Adapt the discourse to the audience

- Know and understand what they can and cannot handle

- Apply the subject material to the audience

Labora Books

an imprint of Saint Benedict Press

Labora Books gives voice to the next generation of Catholic writers. We publish fiction and nonfiction from new authors as well as special works from established authors addressing well-defined audiences within the Church.

Labora Books is an imprint of Saint Benedict Press, a Catholic publisher founded in Charlotte, NC in 2006. The company's name pays homage to the guiding influence of the Rule of Saint Benedict and the Benedictine monks of Belmont Abbey, North Carolina, just a short distance from the company's headquarters in Charlotte, NC.

Saint Benedict Press is the parent company for a variety of imprints in addition to Labora Books, including TAN Books, Benedict Books, Benedict Bibles, and Catholic Courses. The full Saint Benedict Press catalog includes Bibles, Lives of the Saints, spiritual classics, Catholic fiction, prayer books and devotionals, works of ascetic, dogmatic and mystical theology, and audio and video lectures presented by the best minds of the Church.

For a free catalog from Saint Benedict Press,
visit us online at
saintbenedictpress.com
or call us toll-free at
(800) 437-5876.

Learn More

Catholic Courses is the newest imprint in the Saint Benedict Press family. Catholic Courses shares the riches of our Catholic intellectual heritage through audio and video lectures presented by the best minds of the Church. Courses are offered in six categories—History, Philosophy, Scripture, Literature, Saints, and Theology. Courses are enhanced with exciting and informative visual aids and accompanied by course guidebooks. Each course is engaging, relevant, faithful, and provides a gateway to the Catholic intellectual tradition.

Perfect for in-home education, classroom settings or parish groups, Catholic Courses is easy to get started, with no "prerequisites" or prior education needed. All courses are available in both audio and video formats. Whether you are a parent, teacher or catechist, you will want to take full advantage of these tremendous resources to Learn More.

For a full catalog and free previews
visit us online at
catholiccourses.com
or call us toll-free at
(800) 437-5876

CPSIA information can be obtained at www.ICGtesting.com
Printed in the USA
BVOC011708200911

271527BV00012B/1/P